Colin McNaughton is a renowned poet and is recognized as one of Britain's leading children's authors and illustrators. He has produced over seventy books, including *Have You Seen Who's Just Moved in Next Door to Us?* (winner of the Kurt Maschler Award), *Jolly Roger* (winner of the British Design Production Award for Children's Books) and *Potty Poo-Poo Wee-Wee!* He is also the author of a popular series of humorous poetry that includes the collections *Wish You Were Here (And I Wasn't)* and *Making Friends with Frankenstein.*

Colin lives in London with his wife and two sons.

Books by the same author

CAPTAIN ABDUL'S
PIRATE SCHOOL

*For Rocky Lawson,
the first pirate I ever met*

First published 1994 by Walker Books Ltd
87 Vauxhall Walk, London SE11 5HJ

This Sprinters edition published 2006

Published in hardback by Heinemann Library, a division of
Reed Educational and Professional Publishing Limited,
by arrangement with Walker Books Ltd

© 1994, 2001 Colin McNaughton

This book has been typeset in Garamond 3

Printed and bound in Great Britain by J.H. Haynes & Co. Ltd

British Library Cataloguing in Publication Data:
's available from the British Library

·1-4063-0611-8
4063-0611-8

rbooks.co.uk

CAPTAIN ABDUL'S
PIRATE SCHOOL

COLIN McNAUGHTON

WALKER
BOOKS

Dear Diary,

Well, here I stinking am! My first stinking day at Captain Abdul's Pirate School. My stinking dad has sent me here because he says I'm a big softie! (Just because I like writing poems and painting pictures!) He says it will toughen me up. He says a kid my age should jump at the chance of becoming a pirate. He says that when he was a kid he wanted to be a pirate and so should I.

He says I should be grateful.

Well, I say, "Nuts!" and I say, "Steaming cowdung!" and I say, "I hope he swallows his pipe!"

P.S. I have a secret.

I have smuggled my little dog Spud in my trunk. He's the only friend I've got in the whole stinking world!

We were met at the door by
Captain Abdul himself: hairy,
scary and with more bits missing
than a second-hand jigsaw.

"Follow me upstairs, me little buccaneers," said Captain Abdul, "an' we'll get yer kit stowed away, ooh-arrgh, that we will. Ha-har, ooh-arrgh!"

Hammocks ~ ooh ~ arrgh!

Later, Captain Abdul took us

Next we were given our school
uniforms and told to introduce
ourselves.

Françoise
du Plonk

Jim
Silver

Ching
Yih

Ali
Khoja

Unfortunately, Spud thought this included him! Luckily the captain likes dogs and said he could stay (for a small fee).

I was a bit nervous about meeting the other kids but they don't seem too bad – they look just as miserable as me.

Tom Tew

Anne Bonney

Frankie Drake

Samuel P. Chop

We then had supper and went to bed, where I wrote this and cried a bit for my mum.

Jack Rackam

Simon Smee

Ben Gunn

Bartholomew Sharp

Mary Read

Beryl Flynn

Dear Diary,

Woke up this morning and stood up in bed. Forgot I was in a hammock – bit of a headache. I was brushing my teeth when Bully-boy McCoy came in.

"What yer doin' that for?" he asked.

Who ever heard of a pirate with nice teeth!

"If I don't, sir, my teeth will go black and fall out," I replied.

"What's wrong with that?" he said. "Who ever heard of a pirate with nice teeth!" And he confiscated my toothbrush!

Today we studied history.
Portobello Billy told us an exciting
story about Calico Jack the pirate,
set in his favourite place –
the West Indies.

Dear Diary,

We were queueing for breakfast this morning when Walker the Plank came over and asked Rosemary Lavender if she was pushing in.

"Yes, sir," admitted Rosemary.

"Well done!" said Walker the Plank and walked away.

Today's lessons were maths and
geography. In maths we learned
about angles. (You use them when
aiming cannon.) In geography we
learned where the West Indies are
and how to read treasure maps.

Dear Diary,

The beastly Captain Abdul has scolded me for being too neat and tidy. He suspects me of brushing my hair –

"Combs an' hairbrushes, the possession of, is a floggin' offence, ooh-arrgh!" he told me.

Today we had arts and crafts. We learned how to make cannon balls, swords, fake money and how to put model ships into rum bottles. (Spanish Omar Lette very kindly emptied the bottles for us.)

Dear Diary,

Last night we were doing our homework when Riff-raff Rafferty came in and caught little Simon Smee copying from another boy.

"Was you cheatin', boy?" howled Riff-raff.

"Yes, sir," said Simon Smee in a small voice.

"Good boy!" yelled the teacher. "Go to the top of the class!"

Today we learned how to speak pirate. Can't wait till next week's lesson. It's pirate swearwords!

Ooh-arrgh!

Oooo!

Oo-la-la!

O!

Dear Diary,

The teachers had a party last night! They kept coming up and saying it was much too early to be in bed and why weren't we having a midnight feast or rampaging round the town looking for trouble!

"Why, when I was your age," said the captain, "I already had a wooden leg! Ooh-arrgh!"

When he finally woke up today he bellowed, "Fresh air is what we need, ooh-arrgh! We're goin' to sea!"

For the rest of the day we sailed around the harbour in the *Golden Behind*, learning pirate stuff.

Dear Diary,

Tricked! Betrayed! Duped! Fiddled! Fooled and double-crossed! Last night, after I'd taken Spud for a walk, he ran into the staffroom and I followed him in.

From the shadow of the captain's hammock, hidden by clouds of tobacco smoke, I heard terrible things…

"KIDNAP!" I yelled, when I got back to our quarters. "Captain Abdul and his dirty double-crossing teachers are going to kidnap us tonight and when our mums and dads arrive tomorrow for parents' day, all they will find will be a ransom note! We must do something!"

Arrgh!

"But what?" asked the kids.

"MUTINY!" said I. "We get them before they get us!"

"YES!" everyone shouted.

"Shush!" I hissed. "Get your swords and follow me. Tom, you bring the ropes."

"Aye-aye, Captain!" said Tom. "I mean, yes, Pickles."

Armed to the teeth with swords
and ropes, our fearless band of pirate
pupils crept down to the staffroom.

I gave the order and we attacked!

The battle was over in minutes. We swarmed all over the pirate teachers and tied them up with so much rope they looked like cocoons!

We rolled the teachers out onto
the quayside.

One of the kids shouted, "What now?"

"We sail for the West Indies!" I cried.
"Who's with me? Who really wants to
be a pirate?"

"ME! ME! ME!" they all shouted.

"Good!" said I. "Raid the kitchen, fill the water barrels and get the ship ready. We sail in ten minutes!"

I wrote a note to our parents telling them what had happened, pinned it to Captain Abdul and we set sail.

Dear Diary, (six months later)
This is the life! We now call
ourselves "Pirate pirates" because
we only steal from other pirates.

On our last raid we found out that
pirates from all around the world
had heard about our mutiny.

Thinking how well taught we
must have been, they have sent
their kids to Captain Abdul's
school! Abdul claims the mutiny
was all his idea – part of his
teaching plan. The scoundrel!

And so everybody is happy: Captain Abdul because his school is a roaring success and our parents because we send lots of treasure home.

The kids are happy because they get to sail and swim and fight and fire cannon and rob bullies and stay up all night!

And me? Well,
I paint my pictures
and write my poems
and I'm captain of
my own pirate ship!
Who could ask for
anything more...

I'm Captain
Maisy Pickles –
the happiest girl
in the whole, wide,
wonderful world!

Sprinters

Fun Sprinters for you to enjoy!

Captain Abdul's Pirate School	Colin McNaughton
Care of Henry	Anne Fine
Cool as a Cucumber	Michael Morpurgo
Cup Final Kid	Martin Waddell
Ernie and the Fishface Gang	Martin Waddell
Fearless Fitzroy	Kathy Henderson
Fighting Dragons	Colin West
The Finger-eater	Dick King-Smith
The Haunting of Pip Parker	Anne Fine
Impossible Parents	Brian Patten
Jolly Roger	Colin McNaughton
Lady Long-legs	Jan Mark
Molly and the Beanstalk	Pippa Goodhart
Nag Club	Anne Fine
No Tights for George!	June Crebbin
Patrick's Perfect Pet	Annalena McAfee
Posh Watson	Gillian Cross
The Snow Maze	Jan Mark
Star Striker Titch	Martin Waddell
Taking the Cat's Way Home	Jan Mark
Tarquin the Wonder Horse	June Crebbin
Tricky Nelly's Birthday Treat	Berlie Doherty
The Vampire Across the Way	Dyan Sheldon